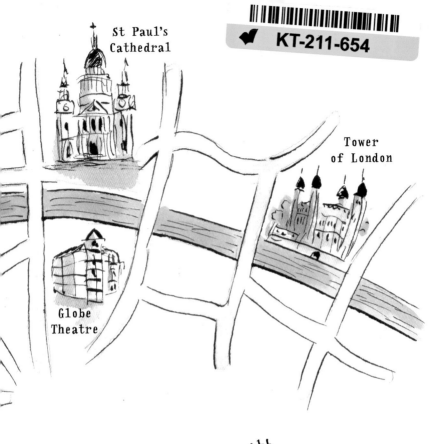

St Paul's Cathedral

Tower of London

Globe Theatre

I live here with my brother Christopher

For Freya, with love.
G.A.

To my own royal family,
Kate, Philippa, Wendy, and Saffy.
T.R.

ORCHARD BOOKS
338 Euston Road, London NW1 3BH
Orchard Books Australia
Level 17/207 Kent Street, Sydney, NSW 2000

First published in 2012 by Orchard Books

ISBN 978 1 40832 005 1

A CIP catalogue record for this book
is available from the British Library.

10 8 6 4 2 1 3 5 7 9

Printed in Italy

Orchard Books is a division of Hachette Children's Books,
an Hachette UK company.

www.hachette.co.uk

Me, the QUEEN and Christopher

by
Giles Andreae

Illustrated by
Tony Ross

ORCHARD

Hello.

I'm Freya and I'm seven.

And something so **AMAZINGLY AWESOME** happened to me recently that I just HAD to write it down in this book.

So, here's my story...

One day I get a letter. It's a very posh-looking letter. It says Buckingham Palace on the back of the envelope. Well, that's a pretty big clue, isn't it?!

Buckingham Palace

I tear it open - and guess what?

It's only from

THE QUEEN!

The actual

QUEEN of ENGLAND!

"Dear Freya," it says. She knows my name!

The Queen of Eng-er-land

actually knows my **NAME!!**

"Dear Freya,

Every year it is my pleasure to invite one British school child for tea at Buckingham Palace. This is most interesting for me because the child is picked quite randomly. This year I would be delighted if YOU would be my guest on Friday the somethingty-something of . . .

Oh,
my
LOLLIPOPS!

Tea with the Queen!

ME!!

So me and Mummy go to get me a new dress. I mean, you need a pretty SPECIAL dress for tea with the Queen, right?

And Mummy and Daddy drop me off at the gates of **ACTUAL** Buckingham Palace. Daddy took the day off work because he thought the Queen might just say hello to him too, but ...

...oh no...just me...Freya!

So these soldiers with huge black furry hats let me in through the gates and I walk right up to the front door. Well, DOORS actually.

A man who looks like a penguin lets
me in and bows.

Then, right there in front of me...
it's **The QUEEN!** In a
REALLY SMART DRESS!

"Hello, Your Royal Majesty-ness," I say.
That's how you talk to the Queen.
And I do a curtsey.

Well, I **TRY** to do a curtsey, but actually my feet get a bit tangled up ... and I slip.

And my head hits the Queen . . . on the knee . . . quite hard.

"Oh flipp

ety-poo!"

shouts the Queen, and she
straightaway falls down.

It turns out that the Queen
hasn't got very good knees.

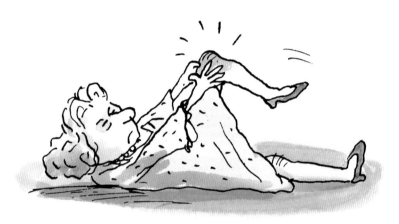

And now she's got a very
sore bottom, too.

The ladies who follow her around don't quite know what to do. I think they're a bit frightened of pulling up her dress to see if she's hurt.

But, in the end, that's
EXACTLY what they do.

And I can tell you that the Queen BRUISES very easily. Her bottom is **TOTALLY PURPLE!**
Poor Queen.

I can also tell you that the Queen wears knickers with **DOGS** on them. On Fridays, anyway. And very pretty they are, too.

Anyway, she picks herself
up and takes me upstairs

through about a **million** corridors...

... with **HUGE** pictures of
scary-looking old people in them ...

... and finally we get to what she calls her "private quarters".

Well, the Queen's "private quarters"
(I think that means the bit where she actually
LIVES) are COMPLETELY different to the
rest of the palace.

To be honest, they're quite tatty. "Lived-in",
I think is what my mummy calls it.

The wallpaper is a bit peely, but LOVELY
and pretty, with old-fashioned flowers all over
it. And there's an ironing board in the corner
with a stack of pants just sitting there.
It's actually quite like my gran's flat.

"Sorry," says the Queen as she sees me looking at the pants. "He says no one can do them like I can. I just haven't put them away yet."

"Now ... let's have tea, Freya. What would you like? What's your favourite?"

"I don't know, Your Majesty-ness," I say. "What's yours?"

"Beans on toast," says the Queen, quick as a flash.

"BEANS ON TOAST!" I say. "But you're the Queen! You're meant to eat roast beef, and lobster sandwiches and stuff."

"I know," says the Queen, smiling. "Don't tell anyone." And she winks.

I LIKE
the Queen!

Then she gets a couple of tea bags and plops them into two **GIANT** mugs.

"The secret of a decent cup of tea," she says, concentrating very hard, "is to dip your tea bag in EXACTLY twenty-seven times."

"And you MUST use boiling water."

47

"Sugar?"

"Three, please," I say.

"Oh," says the Queen. "Me, too!"

So we sit down and eat our beans on toast

and we drink our tea.

Then I spot a TV in the corner.
"What do you like to watch?" I say.

"Oh, mainly wrestling," says the Queen,
"but I've just been given the most
AMAZING thing by The King of Tonga.
It's marvellous. I do it every day. You'd
LOVE it."

She starts fiddling with a remote control but nothing happens, so she kicks a black box under the telly.

"Oh flippety-poo," she says. "You try."

She hands me the remote and I press the red button.

Suddenly, music starts blasting from the screen.

"Wait!" shouts the Queen. "I haven't got into my outfit yet."

She scurries off and, moments later,
she appears ...

... in a very comfy-looking tracksuit and a pair of old slippers with a **HUGE** hole in the toe.

"The dogs," she says, apologetically, as she sees me looking.

"Right ... let's do some dancercises!"

"Yes sir, I

sings the Queen along with the telly, copying the moves of the little cartoon person on the screen **VERY WELL INDEED.**

"... Boogie-woogie
ALL NIGHT

OOOOONG!"

Then she spins around and finishes with one
finger pointing right up in the air and a
seriously groovy expression on her face.

59

Then something happens that I'm not sure I can even tell you about.

But actually you have bought this book, so probably I should.

Well, you know what happens when you eat a lot of beans?

Yup, just when the Queen finishes dancing
and the music goes completely quiet, she
actually does the most **ENORMOUS** ...

Well, I'm not going to **ACTUALLY SAY IT, AM I?** But trust me... it was **IMPRESSIVE**.

"Safety," says the Queen.

"Go Queen!!" I say. Well, I couldn't ignore it, could I?

I try to do a high five with her, but I'm not sure she knows what that is. So I just pretend I'm waving and I think I get away with it.

"What a lot of photos," I say, looking round the walls.

"They're all of my family," says the Queen,
puffing a little bit, hands on her knees. "Come
and have a look."

"That's my eldest grandson," she says proudly, "and his GORGEOUS wife. On their wedding day."

"She's **BEAUTIFUL!**" I say.

"Isn't she?" says the Queen, with a lovely smile. "Tell me about YOUR family."

"Well, I've got a brother," I say.

"Oh," says the Queen. "Have you got a photo of him?"

"Yes," I say. I reach into my pocket. "I **ALWAYS** carry a photo of him. He's called Christopher."

The Queen looks at the photograph. Then she looks straight at me.

"Oh," she says.

Then, "He's BEAUTIFUL, too."

"Yes." I smile. I **LOVE** my brother. "And he's **VERY** funny!"

We look at each other. The Queen has really kind eyes.

"Does he like cupcakes?"

"He LOVES cupcakes!" I say.

"How do you know?"

"I can tell," says the Queen, just like that.
"I love cupcakes, too. Let's make him some."

So, the Queen, right in her own kitchen, in her "private quarters", gets out butter, sugar, flour, eggs ... all the usual stuff.

And then she opens this secret cupboard and suddenly starts saying ...

"chocolate powder,

caramel,

fudge,

toffee,

strawberry sauce,

sherbet stars,

sugary sprinkles . . ."

and it turns out that she's just an absolute **EXPERT** in **EXACTLY** the kind of cupcakes that Christopher **ADORES!**

WHAT A DAY!!

So, in the end, I take this **HUGE** box of cupcakes, I say goodbye to the Queen, I curtsey (without falling over), and my mum and dad pick me up at the gates.

"Has she gone back inside, then?" asks my dad, looking around.

"Yes, Daddy," I say.

Two weeks later, our whole school and, as it turns out, about a thousand million other people, go to London to watch the Queen passing by in a **HUGE** procession. It's a **VERY IMPORTANT DAY**.

I'm with Mum and Dad and Christopher. And, because of Christopher's wheelchair, we're right at the back of the crowd.

The Queen looks **AMAZING**. She's in another absolutely **BEAUTIFUL** dress. She's looking around doing her posh wave.

Suddenly, her hand stops.
She looks **RIGHT AT ME**. She smiles.

Then she has a word with her footmen. The
entire procession stops. Very slowly, the
Queen steps out of her carriage. Hey, I know
how sore her bum must be.

Oh flippety-poo!

She's heading
straight for **ME**!

Dad looks so nervous that I think
he's going to be sick.

"Hello, Freya," says the Queen.

"And you must be Christopher." She gives him an **ENORMOUS** smile. "Did you like the cupcakes?"

I don't know if I can describe what
Christopher does next. But he makes this
kind of face. And it's the kind of face
that makes the Queen bend down...
and just HUG him.

"Have you ever been in a carriage?" she says.

Christopher thinks for a bit. Then he makes one of his really excited noises and throws his head from side to side like he's nearly going berserk.

"This ..." he says, stabbing the arm of his wheelchair with his finger again and again. "... this my CARRIAGE!"

The Queen smiles ... then laughs ...
then really laughs out loud so that
EVERYONE can hear.

"Freya said you were funny," she says,
squeezing his hand. "But that's brilliant,
Christopher. Brilliant!"

Then she whispers something in this footman's ear (quite how he can hear it through his massive wig I DO NOT KNOW).

But **ALL** the footmen come over and they **LIFT** Christopher **IN HIS WHEELHAIR** high up off the street

and RIGHT into the carriage that the **QUEEN of ENG-ER-LAND** is actually processing through the streets in!!

Well, what can I say about Christopher?
It was the happiest moment of his
ENTIRE life.
And I'm pretty sure it always will be.

But, you know, the Queen is MY friend.
And I think I know her well enough now to say
that it might just **POSSIBLY** have been
the **HAPPIEST DAY** of her life, too.

THE END

(Well, that's ALWAYS what you write at the end of a book, isn't it? Just so people know ...)